Being Kind

By Janine Amos and Annabel Spenceley

Consultant Rachael Underwood

CHERRYTREE BOOKS

A CHERRYTREE BOOK

This edition first published in 2007
by Cherrytree Books, part of
The Evans Publishing Group Limited
2a Portman Mansions
Chiltern Street
London W1U 6NR

Printed in China

Amos, Janine
    Being kind. - Rev. ed. - (Growing up)
    1. Kindness - Pictorial works - Juvenile literature
    I. Title
    177.7

ISBN 9781842344880

CREDITS
Editor: Louise John
Designer: D.R.ink
Photography: Gareth Boden
Production: Jenny Mulvanny

Based on the original edition of Being Kind published in 1997

With thanks to: Owen Martins-Beades, Amrit Vernon, Joshua Lock, Giselle Kandekore,
Kayleigh Goodenough, Corey Heath, Ishani Jobanputra-Uddin, Scarlett Mills-Zivanovic, Kieron Cox-Henry

First Day

Pink. Green. Blue. Orange.

4

Everyone's busy painting.

It's Owen's first
day at school.
How does Owen feel?

"Where can I work?"
Owen wonders.

Giselle looks up. She sees Owen.

She smiles at him.

Giselle puts down her brush. "I'll show you where the things are," she says.

"Here's the paper," says Giselle.

"And here's an apron."

Giselle helps Owen to
put on his apron.

"You can work next to me," says Giselle.

Kayleigh hurries across. "You found everything!" she says.

"Giselle showed me,"
Owen tells her.

Dressing Up

Here is the dressing up box.

The children are dressing up.

"I'm a pirate!" laughs Ishani.

Corey looks at her.

"I'm a wizard!"
calls Scarlett.

Corey feels worried.

Kieron pulls on a green cloak.

"I'm a dragon!" he shouts.
"Grr! Grr!"

Ishani watches Corey.

Corey is scared.

Ishani goes over to Corey.

She stands right next to him.

Ishani takes hold of Corey's hand.

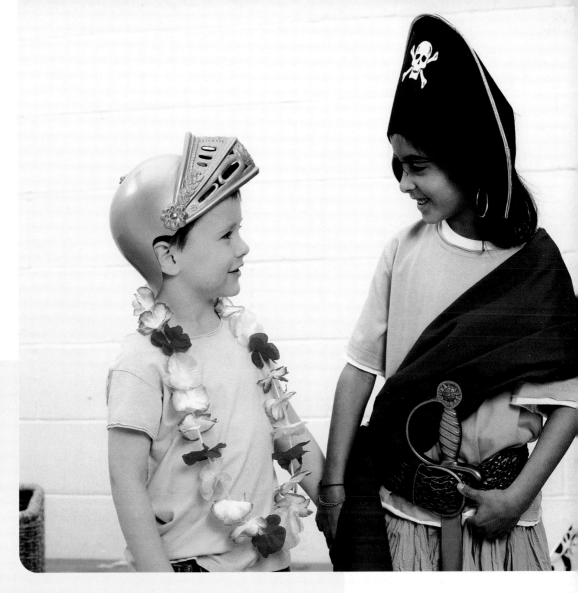

She smiles at Corey.
And Corey feels safe.

Teachers' Notes

The following extension activities will assist teachers in delivering aspects of the PSHE and Citizenship Framework as well as aspects of the Healthy Schools criteria.

Specific areas supported are:

- Framework for PSHE&C 1a, 1b, 2a, 2c, 3a, 4a, 4b, 5d, 5f, 5g
- National Healthy School Criteria 1.1

Activity for *First Day*

Read the story to the children.

- Ask the children to remember all the things Giselle did that were kind.
- Ask them to think of as many ways of being kind to other children in their class as they can. This might include picking up someone's coat if it falls on the floor, or passing the pencil pot when someone asks for it.
- Write the answers on the board with drawings if needed.
- Give each child a 10cm square of paper and ask them to draw something they could do to be kind in their class.
- When the children have finished, mount each drawing on a larger sheet of coloured paper with one line of explanatory text written by the artist.
- Staple together all the drawings to make a quick and simple book.
- Alternatively, use a digital camera to take pictures of children acting out the 'kind acts'. Print out the pictures and add one line of text to each picture to make the book.

Activity for *Dressing Up*

Read the story to the children.

- Sitting in a circle introduce the children to a teddy bear (perhaps one that is already in the class) and explain that Teddy is very upset or scared, lonely, angry etc. today.
- Ask the children to guess why and then they can ask Teddy if this is correct.
- Make Teddy shake his head until you have the answer you were looking for. Perhaps someone has been unkind to him, or someone didn't want to play with him.
- When the children have guessed the answer, ask them to think of a way they could help Teddy feel better. What could they say or do?
- Pass Teddy round the circle and let each child say or do whatever they can to make Teddy feel better. For example they could suggest an invitation to play, a hug, tell a joke or make a kind comment.
- At the end of the circle ask Teddy how he feels now and have him be happy again.
- Ask the children to try to remember all the kind things they suggested to make Teddy feel better.
- List these with drawings where appropriate and pin to the classroom wall. Label the display: 'We are kind to each other'.
- After each playtime for the rest of the week, ask the children to identify any of the kind actions on the list that they have completed.